IDAHO

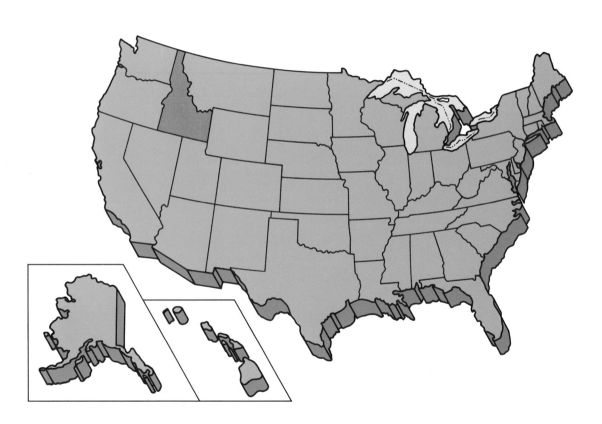

IDAHO

Kathy Pelta

Lerner Publications Company

LIBRARY OF CONGRESS
CATALOGING-IN-PUBLICATION DATA
Pelta, Kathy.
   Idaho / by Kathy Pelta.
      p.   cm. — (Hello USA)
   Includes index.
   ISBN 0-8225-2734-0 (lib. bdg.)
   1. Idaho—Juvenile literature. I. Title II. Series.
F746.3.P45   1994
979.6—dc20   94-2235
                                      CIP
                                       AC

Cover photograph courtesy of Jim Hughes / Idaho Panhandle National Forests.

The glossary that begins on page 68 gives definitions of words shown in **bold type** in the text.

Manufactured in the United States of America
1 2 3 4 5 6 – I/JR – 00 99 98 97 96 95

 This book is printed on acid-free, recyclable paper.

CONTENTS

Did You Know . . . ?

☐ The world's largest potato chip is at the Potato Museum in Blackfoot, Idaho. The chip measures 14 feet (4 meters) by 25 feet (8 m).

☐ One of the largest diamonds ever found in the United States, nearly 20 carats, was uncovered near McCall, Idaho.

☐ In 1974 daredevil Evel Knievel tried to leap across the Snake River canyon in Idaho on his rocket-powered motorcycle. He didn't make it because his safety parachute opened too soon. Knievel floated to the ground and was not seriously injured.

❏ Balanced Rock near Buhl, Idaho, stands 40 feet (12 m) high on a base that's only a few feet thick.

❏ The world's first chairlift for skiers began operating in 1936 at the Sun Valley resort in Idaho. Engineer Jim Curran based his design on the device he had invented to load bananas onto ships—only instead of hooks, he used chairs.

❏ At Hagerman Fossil Beds in southern Idaho are fossils of ancient horses, camels, and other animals that lived between two and three million years ago.

❏ On August 13, 1896, outlaw Butch Cassidy robbed the Bank of Montpelier in Idaho of more than $7,000. A replay of the shoot-out that occurred is held every summer on Montpelier's Main Street.

A Trip Around the State

Idaho is a state of surprises and contrasts. It has prairies and mountains, lava flows and sand dunes, ice caves and hot springs. White-water rivers tumble through steep canyons, and thick evergreen forests surround mountain lakes. Some of the state's wilderness areas have no roads and can only be explored on foot, on horseback, or by river raft. Several streambeds have been mined for gold and silver, as well as dozens of varieties of gemstones—which is why one of Idaho's nicknames is the Gem State.

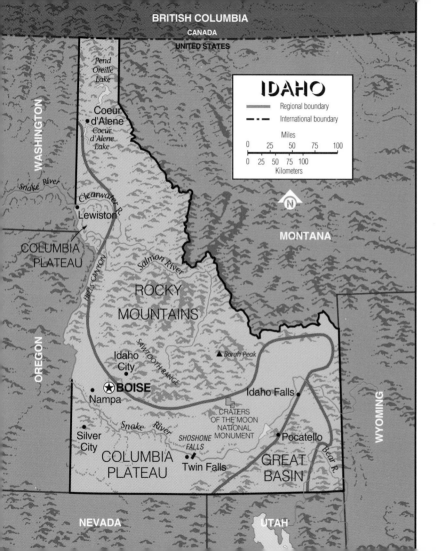

On a map, Idaho looks something like a cabin with a bumpy roof and a lopsided chimney. Long and narrow, the chimney is often called the panhandle, since it resembles the handle of a frying pan.

To the west, beyond the neighboring states of Washington and Oregon, lies the Pacific Ocean. For this reason, Idaho is called a Pacific Northwest state.

Across the mountains to the east are Montana and Wyoming. Nevada and Utah are Idaho's southern neighbors. To the north lies British Columbia, a province of Canada.

Idaho has three main land regions—the Rocky Mountains, the Columbia Plateau, and the Great Basin. The Rocky Mountain region covers three-fourths of the state, stretching from the panhandle to southeastern Idaho. Part of a huge mountain system, the Rockies run from Canada to New Mexico.

The Sawtooth Range in central Idaho is part of the Rocky Mountain region.

11

The Rockies were formed millions of years ago, when massive rocks shoved up through the earth's crust. Thick sheets of ice called **glaciers** later carved valleys into the mountains. Borah Peak, Idaho's highest point, soars 12,662 feet (3,859 m) above sea level. As the glaciers melted, they filled hollow areas and created numerous lakes, including Pend Oreille and Coeur d'Alene. Rivers such as the Salmon and the Clearwater gradually cut deep canyons in the land.

Great flows of hot volcanic lava once oozed through cracks in the earth. When it hardened into rock, the lava formed a vast **plateau,** or highland, called the Columbia Plateau. Part of this plateau extends across southern Idaho.

On the Columbia Plateau, Shoshone Falls plunge 212 feet (65 meters) over a rock cliff on the Snake River.

At Craters of the Moon *(inset)*, a national monument on the Columbia Plateau *(above)*, visitors can explore eerie lava formations and cool, damp caves formed by volcanic flows.

13

The Snake River, named for its many twists and turns, arcs across the Columbia Plateau. The waters of the Snake and its many branches have been channeled to fields of grain and vegetable crops. This system of **irrigation** has made Idaho an important food-producing state.

Hot and cold mineral springs bubble up from underneath the Columbia Plateau. The waters of Warm Springs, near the capital city of Boise, are pumped into pipes to heat some homes.

Volcanoes helped create Idaho's smallest region—the Great Basin. Part of a much larger region that stretches across Utah and Nevada, the Great Basin has flat, sandy plains and grassy plateaus. Mountain ranges in Idaho's Great Basin reach as high as 9,000 feet (2,743 m). The Bear, the main river in the region, flows southward into Great Salt Lake in Utah.

Wheat is raised in some parts of the Great Basin.

14

Although Idaho sits on the Canadian border, the state's high mountains block out the cold winds and blizzards that sweep southward from Canada. Warm breezes blow east across the state from the Pacific Ocean.

Valleys are the warmest spots in Idaho, while mountain towns are the coolest. Summer days can be hot, reaching 90° F (32° C) or more in some places. But at night, the thermometer drops to around 50° F (10° C). Winter temperatures range from 10° F (–12° C) to 25° F (–4° C) or more. The mountains and valleys of the panhandle receive the most rain and snow, while the Columbia Plateau and the Great Basin remain dry throughout the year.

Idaho's rugged mountains offer year-round recreation for outdoor enthusiasts.

Forests of pine, cedar, fir, and aspen trees cover nearly half of Idaho. Deer and chipmunks dart through the woods and meadows. Wilderness areas shelter black bears, cougars, moose, and elks. Surefooted bighorn sheep and Rocky Mountain goats climb the mountainsides. Lizards and rattlesnakes slither among the sagebrush in the state's dry regions.

Idaho's deep lakes and rushing streams hold a wide variety of fish, including salmon, trout, and sturgeon. Along a rugged canyon of the Snake River, golden eagles, hawks, and falcons nest in a national refuge for birds of prey.

16

From dry sagebrush *(facing page)* to thick forests *(above),* Idaho has a great variety of plant life. Mountain goats *(upper right)* and moose *(lower right)* are found in the state's cooler areas.

Idaho's Story

The first people to settle in what is now Idaho were hunters, who arrived while searching for game about 13,000 years ago. On the walls of the caves they lived in, these people painted, carved, and scratched pictures of hunters and their prey, which included mammoths and giant bison. The descendants of these hunters are called Native Americans, or American Indians.

The largest and most powerful Indian group in what is now Idaho called itself Ne-Mee-Poo, meaning "the people." French fur traders who arrived much later called these Indians the Nez Perce. Like the Coeur d'Alene, the Kalispel, the Kootenai, and other tribes in the northern and central mountains, the Nez Perce lived along river valleys. In the dry lands to the south lived the Shoshone, the Bannock, and the Paiute Indians.

The Snake River cut Hells Canyon *(facing page)*, the deepest gorge in North America. Indians in the area knew this rugged terrain well.

18

In southwestern Idaho *(below)*, ancient people carved pictures onto the sides of cliffs.

19

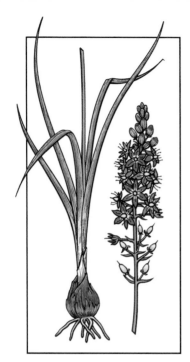

Indians throughout what is now Idaho gathered camas lily bulbs, which look like onions and taste something like sweet potatoes.

All of the nations, or tribes, in what is now Idaho traded with other groups to the east and west. They fished for salmon and hunted game, but their main source of food was the bulb of the blue-flowered camas lily. Using sharp sticks, the Indians dug up the bulbs, dried them, and ground them into flour for cooking.

In the 1700s, the Nez Perce and the Shoshone began trading with other groups for horses. On horseback, the Indians crossed the Rocky Mountains to hunt bison on the Great Plains, hundreds of miles to the east. From the Plains Indians they learned to construct leather tepees and to make pemmican from dried bison meat.

In the early 1800s, the U.S. government sent the explorers Meriwether Lewis and William Clark to find a route west to the Pacific Ocean. By 1805 the men had reached the Rocky Mountains in what is now Idaho. They rested at a Nez Perce village for a month before continuing their journey to the Pacific Ocean.

Horses were unknown to the Indians in what is now Idaho until the 1700s, after Spaniards had brought them to North America. Horses changed the lifestyle of many Indians, including the Nez Perce shown here.

The Lewis and Clark expedition reached what is now Idaho in 1805. They were the first white people to visit the region.

When they returned home, Lewis and Clark reported that many beavers lived in what they called the Oregon Country. This region included what are now Washington, Oregon, and Idaho, as well as parts of Montana and Wyoming.

Some members of the Lewis and Clark expedition stayed in the mountains to trap beavers.

Trappers known as mountain men faced harsh winters, grizzly bears, and other hazards. Many of them died or left the area, unable to survive the dangers. Those who remained earned good money for their beaver pelts, which were used to make expensive top hats for gentlemen.

The United States and Great Britain both claimed the region where the mountain men worked. In 1809 David Thompson, a British explorer and mapmaker, built a trading post on Pend Oreille Lake. Called Kullyspell House, it was the first post in what is now Idaho.

The next year, U.S. trappers started a trading post farther south, on a fork of the Snake River. At these posts, mountain men and Indian trappers traded beaver furs for supplies such as salt, flour, sugar, blankets, and gunpowder.

Mountain men worked alone, trapping beavers in the woods.

To protect their trading posts in the Oregon Country, the United States and Great Britain each built strongholds. Nathaniel Wyeth, a U.S. businessman from Boston, built Fort Hall on the Snake River in 1834. The Hudson's Bay Company, a British fur company, set up Fort Boise on the Boise River.

Religious teachers called **missionaries** were soon arriving to instruct the Indians about Christianity. A band of Nez Perce guided Protestant missionaries Henry and Eliza Spalding to Lapwai, along the Clearwater River. There the Spaldings built a house and a mission school.

Henry Spalding persuaded many Nez Perce to give up their traditional beliefs and customs, including their style of dress and hair. Those who would not change were whipped, which caused many Nez Perce to turn against Spalding, forcing him to leave the region.

Farther north, a Catholic priest named Pierre-Jean De Smet built the Cataldo Mission in 1842

Henry Spalding

to teach the Coeur d'Alene Indians who lived in the area about the Catholic faith. Some of these Indians helped build the mission. It still stands and is the oldest building in Idaho.

De Smet chose the site for the Cataldo Mission in northern Idaho.

At the same time, U.S. explorers Kit Carson and John C. Frémont were mapping a trail used by fur trappers along the Snake River. Their 1843 expedition proved that a safe journey across the dry Columbia Plateau was possible.

Soon settlers were driving covered wagons along this path, which became known as the Oregon Trail. Moving at the rate of about 12 miles (19 kilometers) a day, they stopped at Fort Hall and Fort Boise to rest, repair their wagons, and buy supplies. At Soda Springs, the thirsty travelers drank water that bubbled up from the ground.

In 1846 the United States and Great Britain signed a **treaty**, or agreement, to split the Oregon Country between them. The United

In the 1840s wagon trains began passing through what is now Idaho. At the Three Island Crossing, the Snake River was shallow enough for wagons to ride through the water. Some pioneers wrote their names on large rocks along the trail (inset).

States took control of land south of what is now the border between the United States and Canada. Two years later, the United States named its possession the Oregon Territory.

U.S. officials met with Nez Perce leaders in 1855 to convince them to give up much of their homeland and settle on a **reservation** in what is now central Idaho. The Native Americans knew that if they didn't sign the treaty, the U.S. government would probably force them to give up all of their homeland, so they agreed to the deal. The Nez Perce were paid less than eight cents an acre for their land, but they were told that non-Indians would not be permitted on the reservation.

27

This promise, however, was soon broken. In 1860 a prospector discovered gold on reservation land at Orofino Creek. Shortly afterward fortune hunters began arriving from all over the world.

The newcomers took steamships up the Columbia and Snake rivers as far as the Clearwater River. The miners then walked or rode horses into the hills and raised tents on Nez Perce land. The town of Lewiston became a bustling supply center for the gold seekers. Sawmills cut lumber for buildings and for mining operations. Stables and stores sold horses and everyday goods.

Lewiston sprang up overnight after gold was discovered. At first, many of the buildings were tents.

The prospectors asked the U.S. government to move the boundaries of the Nez Perce reservation so the gold wouldn't be on the Indians' land. Not one of the Nez Perce leaders thought the request was fair—it broke the treaty they had recently signed. But they couldn't stop miners from trespassing, and some of the leaders eventually signed another treaty that made the reservation smaller.

With gold discoveries bringing in more and more people, the U.S. government voted to make this new area of wealth a separate territory. On March 4, 1863, President Abraham Lincoln signed a bill creating the Idaho Territory.

What's in a Name?

Many stories have been told about how Idaho got its name. But most historians believe that Idaho doesn't mean anything in any language. The name first appeared in 1860, when the steamboat *Idaho* began carrying gold seekers up the Columbia River to Lewiston. The owner of the steamboat had gotten the name from a Colorado miner, who said it was an Indian word meaning "gem of the mountains."

People started calling the gold mines near Lewiston the Idaho mines, and the name Idaho was chosen for the territory and eventually for the state. Not until the 1950s did people learn that the miner's story about the Indian meaning was a fake.

Chief Joseph, a Nez Perce leader, wanted to stay on his homeland in Oregon's Wallowa Valley instead of moving to a reservation in central Idaho. The U.S. Army chased him and his people through the mountains of Idaho and Montana before cold and hunger forced him to surrender. In a famous speech he said, "I will fight no more forever."

Meanwhile, non-Indians had begun to settle on the homelands of the Bannock and the Shoshone. The newcomers planted crops, raised livestock, and dug the first irrigation ditches in the region. They also shot the buffalo these Indians depended on for food and clothing. To defend their hunting grounds, the Indians burned grass to starve the settlers' livestock. They also attacked farmers and wagon trains.

To stop these attacks, the U.S. government sent in troops. In one case in 1863, the soldiers surrounded a Shoshone camp and killed more than 200 Indians. A few years later, the Shoshone signed a treaty and agreed to move to the Fort Hall reservation.

The Bannock also agreed to settle on the Fort Hall reservation as long as they could still gather camas bulbs each summer. When settlers let their hogs root out the bulbs, fighting erupted. U.S. troops defeated the Indians in what became known as the Bannock War of 1878.

Reservation Life

Shoshone and Bannock Indians agreed to settle on the Fort Hall reservation *(below),* which was too small to allow them to continue to hunt and gather food. Instead they learned to farm and depended on meager food supplies from the U.S. government. In 1880 a group of Shoshone *(left)* from Idaho's Lemhi reservation traveled to Washington, D. C. There, they signed a treaty that eventually allowed them to move to the more fertile land of the Fort Hall reservation.

After the conflict ended, settlers claimed most of Idaho's rich farmland. During the 1870s, railroad tracks were laid across the territory, and freight trains began carrying crops and livestock to markets in the Midwest. Passenger trains brought in more settlers.

By this time, most of Idaho's gold had been mined. But a new rush began when silver was discovered in the 1880s. Large companies bought land and hired workers to mine the silver, lead, and zinc found in the hills around Coeur d'Alene, in Idaho's panhandle.

With miners and farmers moving to Idaho, the population of the territory grew rapidly. In 1889 residents wrote a **constitution** (set of laws), and on July 3, 1890, Idaho became the 43rd state.

When Idaho became a state in 1890, most people were either farmers *(above)* or miners *(far right)*. Among the non-Indian population were many Chinese people, including this vegetable merchant in Idaho City *(right)*.

Idaho's state flag shows the state seal, which was adopted in 1891. On the seal are symbols of Idaho's wealth from mining and from agriculture. The woman stands for justice, liberty, and equality with men.

Farmers and miners prospered in the new state, but trouble soon developed in the Idaho panhandle. To fight for better wages and working conditions, many of the miners had joined **labor unions** (workers' organizations). After the price of silver fell in 1892, mine owners tried to cut the wages they paid their workers. When union miners protested, mine owners replaced them with non-union employees. This led to fighting between union and non-union miners.

During another union protest in 1899, hundreds of miners set off an explosion at the Bunker Hill mine. Governor Frank Steunenberg called in U.S. troops, who arrested the miners. For the next two years, no miner could work without a permit saying he had not helped dynamite the Bunker Hill.

UNION LEADERS VICTORIOUS

July 27, 1907

Boise, Idaho—After weighing the evidence for nine hours, a jury found Big Bill Haywood not guilty of charges filed against him in the murder of former governor of Idaho Frank Steunenberg. Haywood was one of three union leaders accused of hiring Harry Orchard to carry out the crime. Steunenberg sent U.S. troops to arrest miners who had bombed Idaho's Bunker Hill mine in 1899 after the owners refused to improve working conditions.

Six years later, on a December evening in 1905, the former governor opened his backyard gate, and a homemade bomb exploded and killed him. The murder led to the most famous trial in Idaho's history.

The trial pitted rich mine owners against the struggling union members of the Western Federation of Miners. Newspapers throughout the country followed the case, as Americans watched the headlines.

The prosecution, which brought charges against the union leaders, was led by William E. Borah, a lawyer and U.S. senator from Idaho. For his main evidence, Borah relied on Orchard's confession.

A famous Chicago lawyer named Clarence Darrow defended the union leaders.

As the case unfolded, Darrow skillfully shifted attention away from the specific actions of the union leaders. He focused instead on the good that unions in general were trying to achieve for working-class Americans.

The prosecution, on the other hand, seemed to have clear evidence against the union leaders. But Borah's side of the case suffered a serious blow when he lost the two and only witnesses in support of Orchard's story.

In the end, Darrow's strong attack on mine owners swayed the jury. Their not-guilty verdict caused union leaders throughout the country to rejoice.

Despite the unrest, Idaho's economy continued to grow in the early 1900s. Timbermen began to buy huge forests in northern and central Idaho. Shipping the lumber to eastern markets was expensive, but eventually logging would earn the state more money than mining.

At the same time, dams were built on the Snake River to collect water in **reservoirs,** or pools. During the dry summer months, the water was channeled throughout the Snake River valley to irrigate farmland. Idaho's farmers earned more money than ever during World War I (1914–1918), when food shortages caused the price of crops to rise.

But farmers suffered when prices fell after the war ended and during the Great Depression of the 1930s. During this nationwide economic slump, the price of silver also fell, and the demand for lumber came to a halt. Idaho's workers saw their earnings cut in half. To create jobs for some people, the U.S. government oversaw projects to build roads and raise shelters in state parks. In 1938 workers finished the first paved highway between northern and southern Idaho, easing travel through the mountains.

The Chairman and the Count

During the Great Depression of the 1930s, many workers lost their jobs and poverty was widespread. But some fortunate people still had the time and money to travel. Idaho offered them Sun Valley—the nation's fanciest ski resort.

The resort had been dreamed up by W. Averell Harriman *(left)*, the chairman of the Union Pacific Railroad. Harriman was trying to figure out a way to attract new passengers. Skiing was becoming popular, so Harriman thought a mountain resort might be the answer.

In 1935 Harriman invited Felix Schaffgotsch, an Austrian count and an expert skier, to the United States. The count agreed to help Harriman choose a place for the resort. Together the two men traveled to the snow-capped peaks of Mount Rainier in Washington. They saw the steep slopes of Yosemite National Park in California, and they visited the dry Wasatch Mountains of Utah. But none of these sites satisfied the count.

Finally, they arrived in Ketchum, Idaho. Nearby was a spectacular valley surrounded by treeless slopes. The snow was deep and powdery—perfect for skiing. There was little wind and plenty of warm sunshine. And at one end of the valley lay the tracks of the Union Pacific Railroad.

The count and Averell Harriman had found Sun Valley. A lodge opened the next year and quickly became a favorite spot for movie stars and other wealthy people. By the 1990s, nearly 150,000 people were vacationing in Sun Valley each year.

Idaho's economy boomed again during World War II (1939–1945). Miners produced metals needed for weapons, farmers provided food, and factory workers turned out airplane parts, guns, and ammunition. Thousands of men and women trained at air bases in Boise, Pocatello, and Mountain Home.

After the war, Pend Oreille Lake became a training site for submarine crews and a testing ground for nuclear submarines. In 1949 the U.S. government built a nuclear

Thousands of sailors trained at the Farragut Naval Station in Idaho during World War II. Some men learned to use snowshoes for assignments in Alaska and Greenland.

reactor testing station in southern Idaho. In 1955 Arco became the first city in the world to get all of its electricity from nuclear power.

By the 1960s, food-processing plants in southern Idaho were canning and freezing the state's fruits and vegetables. Lumber companies in northern Idaho manufactured plywood, wood pulp, paper containers, and other wood products from the state's timber. In Boise, Pocatello, and Coeur d'Alene, factories made computers and other high-tech goods.

Shipping all of these products to markets became much easier in 1975. That year Idaho gained a seaport when the last of several dams was completed along the Snake and Columbia rivers. Ocean-

Dockhands at Lewiston load oceangoing ships with grain and other goods.

going ships could now travel inland as far as Lewiston.

Tourism also became a big business. Hikers, hunters, skiers, and other outdoor enthusiasts visited Idaho's wilderness areas. In these protected zones, strict laws prevented road building as well as mining and logging.

11,000 B.C. — Hunters come to what is now Idaho

A.D. 1750 — Nez Perce and Shoshone acquire horses

1805 — Lewis and Clark reach what is now Idaho

1834 — Fort Hall is built

1855 — U.S. government and Nez Perce leaders sign a peace treaty

1860 — Gold is discovered at Orofino Creek

1878 — Bannock War

1890 — Idaho becomes the 43rd state

Although tourism has grown to be the state's third largest industry, some Idahoans believe the state has protected too much land. They argue that mining and logging in wilderness areas would help the state earn more money. Other people disagree. They say that wilderness visitors help the state's economy just as much by spending money for hotels, outdoor equipment, and guides.

While Idahoans clash over the use of wilderness areas, they share a love of their state's natural beauty. By working to solve their differences, Idahoans are planning a better future for their state.

40

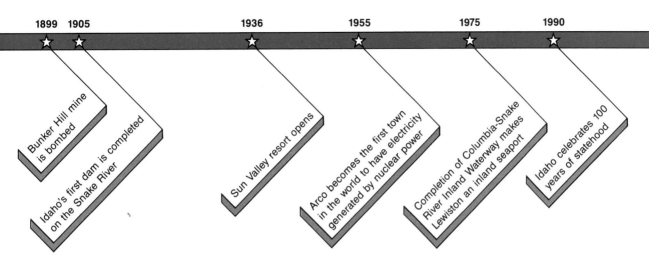

1899   1905   1936   1955   1975   1990

Bunker Hill mine is bombed

Idaho's first dam is completed on the Snake River

Sun Valley resort opens

Arco becomes the first town in the world to have electricity generated by nuclear power

Completion of Columbia-Snake River Inland Waterway makes Lewiston an inland seaport

Idaho celebrates 100 years of statehood

Boise

41

Living and Working in Idaho

For centuries Idaho's rugged landscape kept large numbers of people from settling in the state. But with the discovery of gold in 1860, people braved deserts and mountains to flock to Idaho. Nowadays many Idahoans can trace their roots to these early miners and to the farmers and loggers who followed.

Almost all of Idaho's one million residents were born in the United States. Their ancestors came from Great Britain, Germany, Ireland, the Netherlands, and the Scandinavian countries. About 5 percent of Idahoans are Latinos. Asians and African Americans each number fewer than 1 percent. Many of their ancestors came to Idaho in the late 1800s to mine or to build railroads.

Idaho's past comes to life in the pioneer town of Idaho City, which once bustled with gold seekers.

Nearly 14,000, or 1.4 percent, of the state's population is Native American. About 3,000 Shoshone and Bannock live at the Fort Hall reservation, and 2,000 Nez Perce inhabit the Nez Perce reservation. Other Indians reside in cities or on three smaller reservations. Many practice their traditional religion, study their native language and

Native Americans prepare for a dance competition at a local powwow.

history, and play in traditional sporting events. Throughout the year, various ceremonies are held to honor salmon, berries, and root plants such as the camas lily.

Nearly half of Idaho's people live in the countryside. About one-third have homes in the southwestern part of the state, mostly around Boise—the capital and largest city. Boise and other big towns are located on or near the Snake River. These include Nampa, Twin Falls, Pocatello, Idaho Falls, and Lewiston. Coeur d'Alene is in the Idaho panhandle.

Many buildings from the 1800s still stand in Boise. Visitors can tour Old Fort Boise or the dark cells of the Old Idaho Penitentiary,

Southwestern Idaho is home to a large Basque community, whose ancestors came from Spain to herd sheep.

a prison that once held stagecoach robbers, horse thieves, and other outlaws.

Idaho's many ghost towns are fun to visit. Idaho City and Silver City once bustled with miners. Nowadays visitors can tour weathered buildings, relax in remodeled saloons, and stroll through cemeteries where most of the occupants died from accidents.

History buffs can hike the Lolo Trail, the path Lewis and Clark followed through central Idaho. Farther south, wheel ruts more than 100 years old trace the path of the Oregon Trail, the old settlers' highway. Travelers carved their names and initials into Register Rock, a famous landmark along the trail.

At Logger Days in Cascade, Idahoans test their speed at crosscutting timber the old-fashioned way.

Rodeo action can be found in many Idaho towns.

Festivals and fairs are held in Idaho throughout the year. The Nez Perce perform traditional dances at a powwow in Kamiah. Each March the nation's top cowboys ride and rope at the Dodge National Circuit Finals Rodeo in Pocatello. At Lumberjack Days in Orofino, loggers demonstrate logrolling.

Idaho has two state fairs—the Eastern Fair at Blackfoot and the Western Fair at Boise. Fairgoers enjoy horse races, food, carnival rides, and music. Farmers exhibit their prize cattle, horses, and sheep.

47

More than 1,000 feet (305 m) deep, Pend Oreille Lake in the panhandle is a fisher's paradise.

Idahoans celebrate winter with snow carnivals, ice sculptures, and sled-dog races. Snowmobilers can speed along 5,000 miles (8,045 km) of groomed trails. In January Sun Valley hosts the Duchin Celebrity Invitational Ski Cup Race.

A favorite pastime among Idahoans is fishing. In fact, about one out of every four Idahoans has a fishing license. The Henry's Fork of the Snake River is prized as one of the finest trout-fishing streams in the world.

Another popular sport is whitewater rafting. With thousands of miles of rapids and other white water, Idaho's rivers tempt daredevils. Outfitters offer guided tours down the Salmon and other rough waterways.

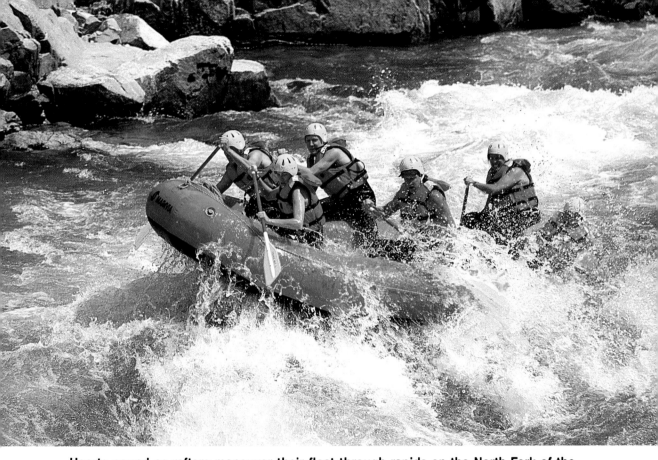

Hearts pound as rafters maneuver their float through rapids on the North Fork of the Payette River.

People from other states come every season of the year to enjoy Idaho's natural beauty. Two-thirds of the state is public land—wilderness areas, national forests, and parks. Rugged mountains have given the state one of its nicknames, Gem of the Mountains. Idaho also boasts natural caves, weird rock formations, and ancient lava beds.

Many Idahoans have jobs helping the state's visitors. Hotel clerks, restaurant workers, and rafting and hunting outfitters all have service jobs, which employ nearly three-fourths of Idaho's workforce. The state's doctors, teachers, and salespeople, as well as its park rangers and other

A park ranger helps a family spot a bird among the cedar trees in the Idaho Panhandle National Forests.

Heaps of potatoes add up to big business in Idaho.

government employees, are also service workers.

In 1889 the University of Idaho was founded in the town of Moscow. Then, as now, many students took classes in agriculture and farm management. Agriculture still earns the state a lot of money and employs about one out of eleven workers.

Nearly one-third of the nation's potatoes come from Idaho, where farmers also grow hay, wheat, barley, and sugar beets. Fruit growers raise apples, cherries, peaches, and pears. Beef cattle and dairy products are also important. Many farmers ship their produce to the Pacific coast by way of the Snake and Columbia rivers.

Some of the state's produce goes to food-processing plants within Idaho for packaging. These and other factories in the state employ about one in seven workers. Around Boise, laborers manufacture electrical machinery, computers, and office equipment.

Throughout the state, timber is an important raw material for manufacturers. Lumber companies process raw timber into plywood, particleboard, wood pulp, and paper. Lumber mills also cut logs to the right shape and size for building cabins and houses.

The state's numerous ghost towns remind people that mining was once Idaho's most important

Logging operations dot roadsides in much of Idaho.

industry. Nowadays, fewer than 3,000 Idahoans (1 percent of the workforce) have jobs in mines. The area around Coeur d'Alene, known as Silver Valley, produces more silver than anywhere else in the world. Lead, zinc, and copper are also mined in this region.

In the southeast, phosphate rock is mined to make fertilizers.

Throughout the state, gemstones such as garnets are found. Whether you call it the Gem State or Gem of the Mountains, Idaho is a jewel in many ways.

After a day at the quarry, a family examines their garnet find with the help of a park ranger.

Protecting the Environment

Fish have long been important to Idaho's people. For centuries Native Americans depended on abundant stocks of salmon as a main food source. Later, settlers built up a fishing industry that thrived on salmon and trout from Idaho's waters. Sportfishing has since become a big attraction for both residents and tourists.

But by the mid-1900s, the numbers of some species, or types, of fish in Idaho began to drop. Commercial fishing crews were hauling in such huge catches that some species couldn't breed fast enough to keep their populations stable or growing. People were polluting rivers and building dams, making it hard for salmon, trout, sturgeon, and other fish to find food and to produce young.

Pollution comes from many different sources. At mines, minerals are separated from rocks in a process that leaves behind lead and other heavy metals. Over time, these waste metals can seep into waterways. During a rainstorm, the chemicals that farmers use on their fields can wash into streams.

Another source of pollution comes from something natural—soil. Trees and grass hold soil in place. But the soil is disturbed when ranchers graze cattle and when loggers cut timber and build roads to get to trees. Even hikers and other people who use land for recreation can loosen soil. Sediment, or dirt, then gradually slides into nearby waterways, making them cloudy.

As the sediment settles to the bottom of a river, it fills spaces between rocks where insects hide. The bugs become trapped and the fish, who feed on the insects, have trouble finding food. Sediment also can bury the gravel beds at the bottom of a waterway, where fish scoop out nests to spawn, or lay

Grazing sheep *(left)* and roads cut into hillsides *(right)* can loosen soil. Eventually, the sediment slides into rivers, where it collects at the bottom.

eggs. When sediment fills a nest, it smothers the eggs. Young fish, who hide at the bottom of a stream, get stuck and can't swim out from between the rocks.

Dams cause the most damage to river life. These cement walls are built to hold back water, some of which is saved to irrigate crops and lawns during the summer. The rest of the water is released gradually to control the speed of the river's flow. This helps prevent flooding during spring snowmelts.

57

Many dams have been equipped to produce hydropower, or electricity generated with water-power. As the water passes through the dam, it sets huge turbines, or engines, in motion. The spinning turbines then power generators that produce electricity. Because the generators don't burn fuel, they don't pollute the air.

Dams provide cheap, nonpolluting electricity and irrigation water. But they also harm fish. By slowing the flow of water, dams slow down fish. This is a big problem for young salmon, called smolts. As smolts mature, they move from fresh water to salt water, travelling from their birth-place in Idaho all the way to the Pacific Ocean.

Before dams, the journey down the Snake and Columbia rivers took 10 days. Now it lasts a month or more. The extra time gives bears and other predators a much better chance of catching smolts for their next meal. Those who do reach the ocean may arrive too late to be able to adapt to life in salt water.

Dams cause many problems for fish.

Dams cause other problems, too. Slow-moving water is warmer than the fish like, so they are more likely to catch diseases. They also get lost more easily without a fast current to direct their journey. Some experts say that 90 percent of all smolts die from turbines, predators, or disease, or simply run out of time to swim to the ocean.

A worker at the Department of Fish and Game collects smolts *(left)* **to raise and breed them in captivity. A salmon** *(below)* **selects a gravel bed for spawning on the Salmon River.**

After a few years in the ocean, salmon return to their birthplace to spawn and die. In 1992 only one sockeye salmon—"Lonesome Larry" *(inset)*—made it to the the lake *(right)* where he was born.

To help save salmon, some Idahoans want to increase the flow of water through dams during the spring, when most smolts swim to the ocean. Others want to decrease the water in reservoirs to make it flow like a natural river and shorten travel time for smolts. Engineers have built bypasses at the dams to catch smolts, which are then put in barges and taken to the ocean.

But barges can't protect fish from all hazards. And it is unlikely that all the people and industries that depend on water for irrigation and for electric power will agree to increase water flow or decrease reservoir levels.

Some Idahoans are working on other projects to improve conditions for the state's fish. Some programs teach people to leave the area along

streams alone, so sediment doesn't get into the water.

To limit the flow of chemicals into rivers, farmers are learning to be more careful about how they apply chemicals to their fields. After a mining job is complete, laws require mining companies to clean up. Rules also set limits on the size and number of certain species of fish anglers can catch and forbid fishing during spawning periods.

With these efforts, Idaho species such as chinook and sockeye salmon, steelhead trout, bull trout, cutthroat trout, and white sturgeon may be saved from extinction. Through careful planning, Idahoans will be able to preserve the state's fish populations now and in the future.

Idaho's Famous People

ACTIVISTS

Joseph R. Garry (1910–1975), a Coeur d'Alene Indian from Plummer, Idaho, served two terms as a state senator in the 1950s and 1960s. From 1953 to 1959 Garry also was president of the National Congress of American Indians, an organization working for the rights of Native Americans.

Morlan Nelson (born 1916) started the Snake River Birds of Prey Natural Area to protect land uniquely suited for peregrine falcons, eagles, and other endangered birds of prey. Nelson has been an active leader at the World Center for Birds of Prey in Boise, where he has lived since 1948.

JOSEPH GARRY ▲

EMMA EDWARDS GREEN ▶

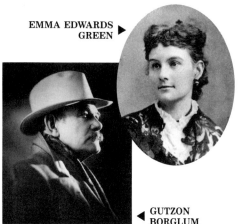

◀ GUTZON BORGLUM

ARTISTS

Gutzon Borglum (1867–1941), a sculptor born near Bear Lake, Idaho, directed a team of workers as they blasted and chiseled Mount Rushmore National Memorial in South Dakota. The 60-foot (18-m) carving features the faces of four U.S. presidents and took 14 years to complete.

Emma Edwards Green (1856–1942) taught painting classes in Boise and in 1891 was asked to enter a competition to design the Idaho state seal. Green's artwork won, making her the first and only woman to design an official state seal.

ATHLETES

Walter Johnson (1887–1946), one of the greatest pitchers in baseball history, was known for throwing a ball so fast it seemed

62

invisible. Johnson played for the Washington Senators for 21 seasons. He was among the first five players to be elected to the Baseball Hall of Fame. Johnson grew up in Weiser, Idaho.

Harmon Killebrew (born 1936), a baseball player from Payette, Idaho, led the American League in home runs four times and in runs batted in three times. After retiring from the Minnesota Twins in 1975, Killebrew became a sportscaster. He was elected to the National Baseball Hall of Fame in 1984.

Picabo Street (born 1971) learned to ski in her hometown of Sun Valley, Idaho. In 1993 Street was ranked among the world's top 10 downhill skiers. In the 1994 Olympics she won a silver medal.

Jackson Sundown (1866–1923) was a Nez Perce horseman from central Idaho. In 1916, at the age of 50, he became the only Indian to win the World Saddle Bronc Riding Championship. He was competing against men who were half his age.

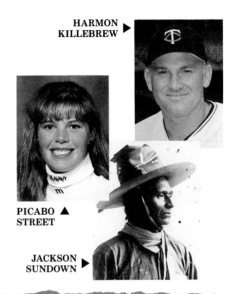

HARMON ▶ KILLEBREW

PICABO ▲ STREET

JACKSON ▶ SUNDOWN

BUSINESS LEADERS

Edwin R. Peterson (born 1921) invented the back-up beeper, which warns people to stay clear of backing vehicles. Peterson made the first Bac-A-Larm in his home basement in Boise. In 1968 he founded Preco, Inc., to manufacture and distribute the alarm and other electronic products.

Jack R. Simplot (born 1909) started the J. R. Simplot Company, a potato-processing empire, at the age of 16. Known as Idaho's Potato King, Simplot created instant potatoes and frozen french fries. Raised in a one-room cabin in Delco, Idaho, Simplot became one of the richest men in Idaho.

EDWIN ▲ PETERSON

◀ JACK SIMPLOT

63

Marion Barton Skaggs (1888–1976), from American Falls, Idaho, bought his father's grocery store in 1915. By 1926 Skaggs was running a chain of more than 400 stores, and the company merged with Safeway grocery stores. Skaggs's leadership helped make Safeway one of the largest food chains in the world.

ENTERTAINERS

Mariel Hemingway (born 1961), from Mill Valley, Idaho, is an actress who has starred in several movies, including *Manhattan*, *Personal Best*, and *Falling from Grace*. She is the granddaughter of the famous writer Ernest Hemingway.

Lana Turner (born 1920), from Wallace, Idaho, was discovered by the movie industry while drinking a soda in a Hollywood drugstore. Among her best-known films are *The Postman Always Rings Twice* and *Peyton Place*.

▲ MARIEL HEMINGWAY

◄ LANA TURNER

FRONTIER FIGURES

C. K. Ah-Fong (1844–1927) left his native China in the 1860s and settled near Boise, where he set up a medical practice and drug shop. Filling a need for qualified doctors, Ah-Fong gained great respect from his patients—white as well as Asian.

Sacajawea (1788–1812?), a Shoshone Indian, was born in what is now eastern Idaho. She helped guide the Lewis and Clark expedition to the Pacific Ocean and served as an interpreter and peacekeeper along the way.

Kitty Wilkins (1849–1936), a horse dealer, started her business at the age of 22 with just one horse. Working out of her family's ranch in Bruneau, Idaho, Wilkins became so successful at

C. K. AH-FONG ▼

KITTY ▲ WILKINS

selling the animals that by the 1890s she had earned a national reputation as Idaho's Horse Queen.

POLITICIANS

William E. Borah (1865–1940), born in Illinois, moved to Boise in 1890 and began practicing law. First elected to the U.S. Senate in 1907, Borah held the position until his death. Borah sided with neither political party. Nicknamed the Great Opposer, he often voted against the ideas of his Republican party colleagues.

Frank Church (1924–1984), born in Boise, was a U.S. senator from Idaho for 24 years. Church chaired the powerful Senate Foreign Relations Committee and the Select Committee on Intelligence. He also worked to preserve Idaho's wilderness.

Gracie Pfost (1906–1965) won the vote of many Idahoans when she successfully led the fight to stop the building of a new dam in Hells Canyon. In 1952 Pfost became the first female Idahoan elected to the U.S. House of Representatives. She grew up on a farm near Boise.

◀ FRANK CHURCH

▲ GRACIE PFOST

WILLIAM BORAH ▶

CAROL RYRIE BRINK ▶

WRITERS

Carol Ryrie Brink (1895–1981), born in Moscow, Idaho, wrote mostly for young people. In 1936 she won the Newbery Medal for *Caddie Woodlawn,* a book based on her grandmother's pioneer life. Altogether, Brink wrote more than two dozen books.

Mourning Dove (1888–1936) was a writer from Bonner's Ferry, Idaho. Part Okanogan and part Colville Indian, she wrote about the lives and folklore of Native Americans in *Coyote Stories* and in *Co-Go-We-A, the Half-Blood.*

65

Facts-at-a-Glance

Nicknames: Gem State, Gem of the Mountains
Song: "Here We Have Idaho"
Motto: *Esto Perpetua* (Let it be perpetual)
Flower: syringa
Tree: western white pine
Bird: mountain bluebird
Gemstone: star garnet

Population: 1,006,749*
Rank in population, nationwide: 42nd
Area: 83,574 sq mi (216,457 sq km)
Rank in area, nationwide: 14
Date and ranking of statehood:
   July 3, 1890, the 43rd state
Capital: Boise
Major cities (and populations*):
   Boise (125,738), Pocatello (46,080),
   Idaho Falls (43,929), Nampa (28,365),
   Lewiston (28,082)
U.S. senators: 2
U.S. representatives: 2
Electoral votes: 4

*1990 census

Places to visit: Silver Valley (Coeur d'Alene mining district), Hells Canyon near Lewiston, Idaho City ghost town, Snake River Birds of Prey Natural Area near Boise, Silent City of Rocks near Alamo, Dinomania in Pocatello, Craters of the Moon near Arco, sand dunes near St. Anthony

Annual events: Winter Carnival in McCall (Jan.–Feb.), Dodge National Circuit Finals Rodeo in Pocatello (March), Cherry Festival in Emmett (June), Paul Bunyan Days in St. Maries (Sept.), Four Nation Powwow in Lewiston (Oct.), Christmas City USA—Lighting Ceremony in Rupert (Nov.)

Natural resources: timber, water, silver, lead, phosphate rock, gold, molybdenum, sand and gravel, limestone, copper, garnets, zinc

Agricultural products: potatoes, hay, wheat, sugar beets, cherries, peaches, beef cattle, milk, trout

Manufactured goods: french fries, canned fruits and vegetables, beet sugar, flour, packaged meats, lumber, particleboard, computers, farm equipment, paper products, fertilizer

ENDANGERED AND THREATENED SPECIES
Mammals—gray wolf, woodland caribou, grizzly bear
Birds—bald eagle, peregrine falcon, whooping crane
Mollusks—Bliss Rapids snail, Idaho springsnail, Snake River physa snail, Utah valvata snail, Banbury Springs limpet, Bruneau Hot Springs snail
Fish—Pacific lamprey, Kootenai River white sturgeon, sockeye salmon, chinook salmon, Bonneville cutthroat trout, burbot
Plants—Macfarlane's four-o'clock, alkali primrose, Howellia aquatilis

WHERE IDAHOANS WORK
Services—52 percent
   (services includes jobs in trade; community, social, & personal services; finance, insurance, & real estate; transportation, communication, & utilities)
Government—19 percent
Manufacturing—15 percent
Agriculture—9 percent
Construction—4 percent
Mining—1 percent

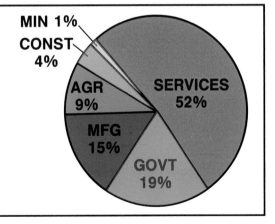

MIN 1%
CONST 4%
AGR 9%
MFG 15%
GOVT 19%
SERVICES 52%

PRONUNCIATION GUIDE

Bannock (BAN-uhk)

Boise (BOY-see)

Borah (BOHR-uh)

Coeur d'Alene (kohr-duh-LAYN)

Kalispel (KAL-uh-spehl)

Kootenai (KOOT-ihn-ay)

Lewiston (LOO-uhs-tuhn)

Nampa (NAM-puh)

Nez Perce (NEHZ PURS)

Orofino (awr-uh-FEE-noh)

Paiute (PY-yoot)

Pend Oreille (pahn-duh-RAY)

Pocatello (poh-kuh-TEHL-oh)

Shoshone (shuh-SHOHN)

Glossary

constitution The system of basic laws or rules of a government, society, or organization. The document in which these laws or rules are written.

glacier A large body of ice and snow that moves slowly over land.

irrigation A method of watering land by directing water through canals, ditches, pipes, or sprinklers.

labor union An organization responsible for improving and protecting the wages, benefits, and general working conditions of workers who pay membership dues.

missionary A person sent out by a religious group to spread its beliefs to other people.

plateau A large, relatively flat area that stands above the surrounding land.

reservation Public land set aside by the government to be used by Native Americans.

reservoir A place where water is collected and stored for later use.

treaty An agreement between two or more groups, usually having to do with peace or trade.

Index

Acknowledgments:

Maryland Cartographics, Inc., pp. 2, 10; Jack Lindstrom, p. 6; Kenneth C. Poertner, pp. 2-3, 7, 8-9, 12, 47, 51, 71; David Dvorak Jr., pp. 9 (inset), 13, 17 (top right); Buddy Mays / Travel Stock, pp. 11, 19 (right), 41, 45, 49, 55, 59 (right); Norma Watts, pp. 13 (inset), 19 (left), 57; Patrick Cone, p. 14; Veda Scherer / Laatsch-Hupp Photo, p. 15; Jerry Hennen, p. 16; Jim Hughes / ID Panhandle Nat'l Forests, pp. 17 (left), 48, 50, 52, 53; ID Parks & Recreation, p. 17 (lower right); ID Hist. Society, pp. 21 (659), 25 (991), 27 inset (815), 31 inset (2377), 32-33 (73.221.417A), 33 left (3796), 35 (2005), 37 bottom (79-124.32), 38 (D60.171.0004), 62 (upper rt. 80-151; middle 71-72.1), 63 (lower right 77-2.45), 64 (lower left 81-2.32; lower right 65-143.1), 65 (middle left 82-2.53; middle right 2252); Denver Public Library, Western History Dept., pp. 22, 26-27, 31; Haynes Foundation Coll., MT Hist. Society, pp. 23, 33 (right); Pacific Univ. Archives, Forest Grove, OR, p. 24; OR Hist. Society #485, p. 28; Smithsonian Institution, Nat'l Anthropological Archives, p. 30; Sun Valley News Bureau / Hist. Photo Coll., Univ. of ID-Moscow, p. 37 top (#5-97-4b); Jim Soyk Jr. / Port of Lewiston, p. 39; Bill Billingham / F-Stock, p. 42; Jim Nau, p. 44; Donna Cutbirth, p. 46; Root Resources: James Blank pp. 54, 60-61, Margaret Crader p. 56; Library of Congress, p. 54 (inset); ID Dept. of Fish & Game, p. 58 (D. Ronayne), 59 (left, D. Ronayne), 61 (inset); Mt. Rushmore Nat'l Memorial, p. 62 (lower left); Greg Griffith, p. 63 (upper left); MN Twins, p. 63 (upper right); Burns Studio, p. 63 (lower left); Nat'l Park Service, Nez Perce Nat'l Hist. Park Coll., p. 63 (upper middle); Hollywood Book & Poster, p. 64 (upper left & right); Boise State Univ. Library, Frank Church Coll., p. 65 (top); Latah Co. Hist. Society, p. 65 (bottom); Jean Matheny, p. 66; Pat Bratvold, p. 69.